THE MAN IN THE IRON MASK

Vol. 6: Musketeers No More

Adapted from the novel by ALEXANDRE DUMAS

THE STORY SO FAR:

In 17th-century France, the famed Three Musketeers—**Athos**, **Porthos**, **and** ~~A~~ramis—were joined in comradeship by young d'Artagnan. Three decades later, Athos ~~h~~ad become a count—Porthos, by marriage, a baron—and shrewd Aramis, the Bishop of ~~V~~annes—while d'Artagnan now captained the King's Musketeers.

Aramis' scheme to put the twin brother of **King Louis XIV** on the throne failed ~~be~~cause its intended beneficiary, Surintendant M. **Fouqet**, would not agree to anything so ~~di~~shonorable. The twin, **Philippe**, was imprisoned, doomed forever to wear an iron mask to ~~co~~nceal his identity. Aramis and Porthos, his unwitting dupe, fled to Belle-Isle. Because of ~~hi~~s divided loyalties, D'Artagnan was removed from leadership of the expedition against them. ~~P~~orthos died defending Aramis—and Aramis fled by boat, hoping to reach Spain.

Meanwhile, Athos mourned for his son, **Raoul**, who had joined a military mission to ~~A~~frica. There, Raoul hoped to find death because of his love for **Louise de la Vallière**, who ~~h~~ad betrayed him to become the King's mistress....

Writer	Special Thanks	Penciler	Inker
Roy Thomas	Deborah Sherer & Freeman Henry	Hugo Petrus	Tom Palmer

Colorist	Letterer	Cover	Special Thanks	Production
~~J~~une Chung	Virtual Calligraphy's Joe Caramagna	Marko Djurdjevic	Chris Allo	Anthony Dial

Assistant Editor	Associate Editor	Editor	Editor in Chief	Publisher
~~Wa~~rren Sankovitch	Nicole Boose	Ralph Macchio	Joe Quesada	Dan Buckley

VISIT US AT
www.abdopublishing.com

Reinforced library bound edition published in 2009 by Spotlight, a division of the ABDO Group, 8000 West 78th Street, Edina, Minnesota 55439. Spotlight produces high-quality reinforced library bound editions for schools and libraries. Published by agreement with Marvel Characters, Inc.

Library of Congress Cataloging-in-Publication Data

Thomas, Roy, 1940-
  The man in the iron mask / adapted from the novel by Alexandre Dumas ; Roy Thomas, writer ; Hugo Petrus, penciler ; Tom Palmer, inker ; Virtual Calligraphy's Joe Caramagna, letterer ; June Chung, colorist. -- Reinforced library bound ed.
    v. cm.
  "Marvel."
  Contents: v. 1. The three musketeers -- v. 2. High treason -- v. 3. The iron mask -- v. 4. The man in the iron mask -- v. 5. The death of a titan -- v. 6. Musketeers no more.
  ISBN 9781599615943 (v. 1) -- ISBN 9781599615950 (v. 2) -- ISBN 978159961596 (v. 3) -- ISBN 9781599615974 (v. 4) -- ISBN 9781599615981 (v. 5) -- ISBN 9781599615998 (v. 6)
  Summary: Retells, in comic book format, Alexandre Dumas' tale of political intrigue romance, and adventure in seventeenth-century France.
  [1. Dumas, Alexandre, 1802-1870.--Adaptations. 2. Graphic novels. 3. Adventure and adventurers--Fiction. 4. France--History--Louis XIII, 1610-1643--Fiction.] I. Dumas, Alexandre, 1802-1870. II. Petrus, Hugo. VI. Title.
PZ7.7.T518 Man 2009
[Fic]--dc22   2008035321

All Spotlight books have reinforced library bindings and are manufactured in the United States of America.

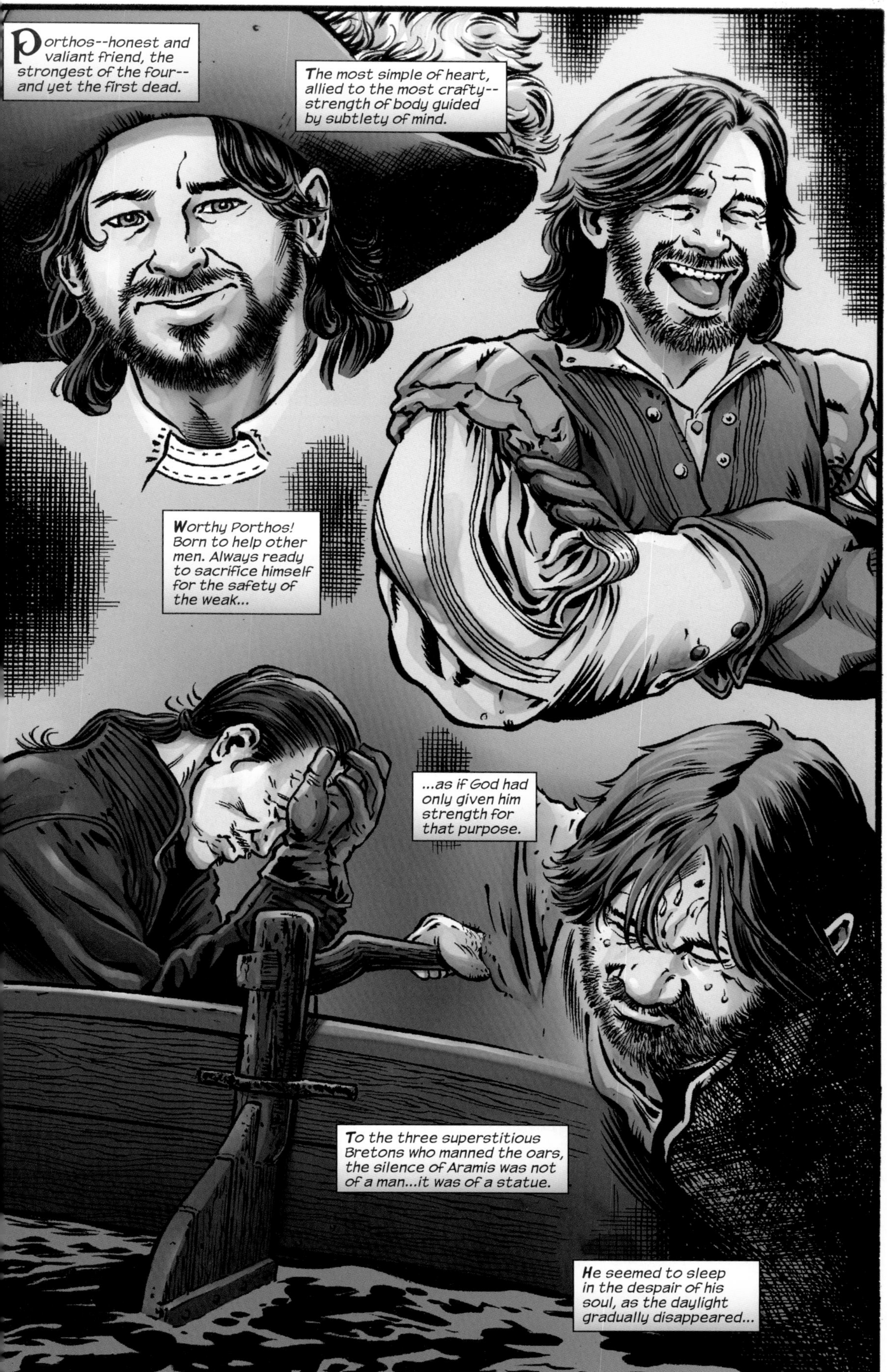
Porthos--honest and valiant friend, the strongest of the four--and yet the first dead.
The most simple of heart, allied to the most crafty--strength of body guided by subtlety of mind.
Worthy Porthos! Born to help other men. Always ready to sacrifice himself for the safety of the weak...
...as if God had only given him strength for that purpose.
To the three superstitious Bretons who manned the oars, the silence of Aramis was not of a man...it was of a statue.
He seemed to sleep in the despair of his soul, as the daylight gradually disappeared...

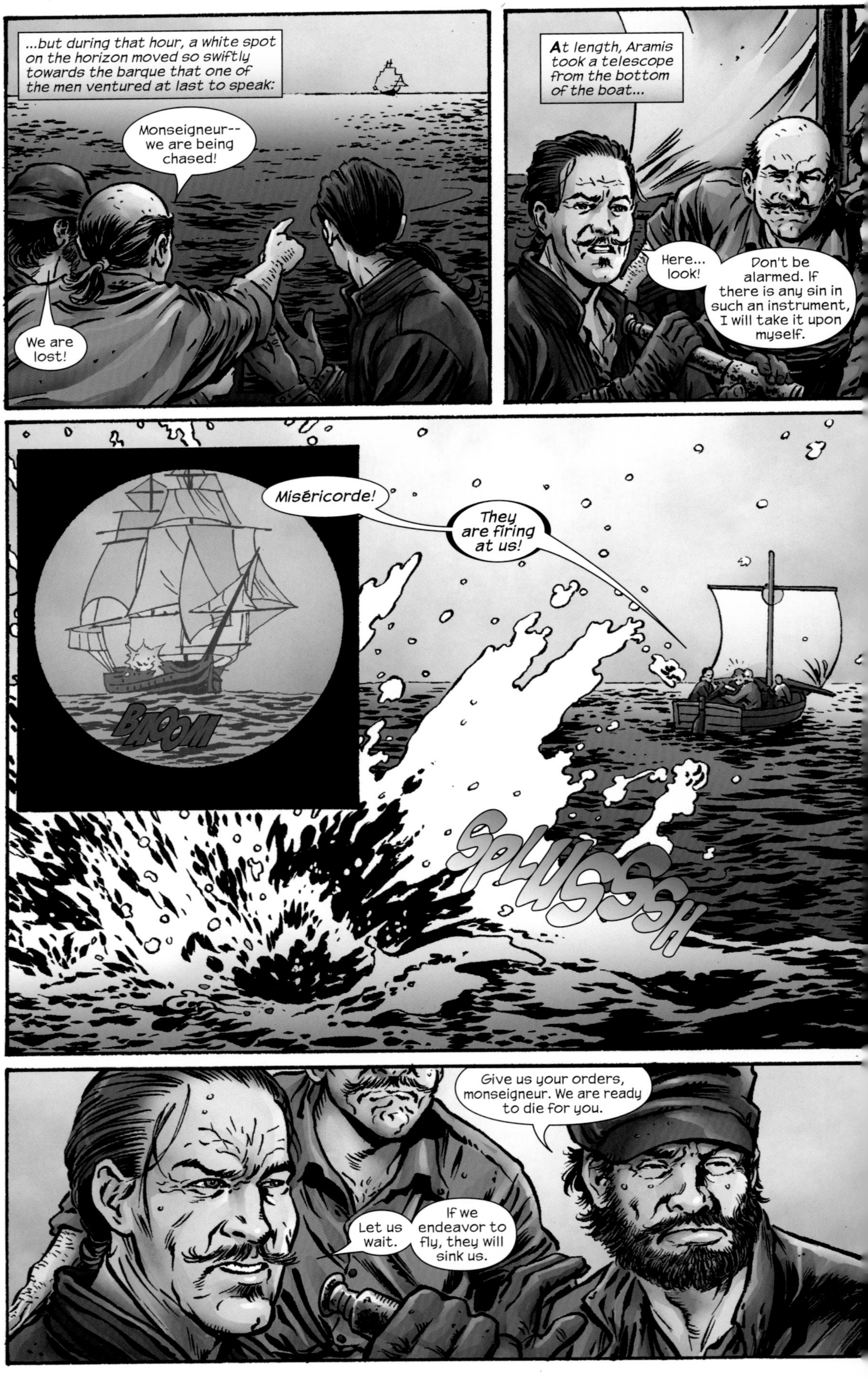
...but during that hour, a white spot on the horizon moved so swiftly towards the barque that one of the men ventured at last to speak:
Monseigneur-- we are being chased!
We are lost!
At length, Aramis took a telescope from the bottom of the boat...
Here... look!
Don't be alarmed. If there is any sin in such an instrument, I will take it upon myself.
BAOOM
Miséricorde!
They are firing at us!
SPLUSSSH
Give us your orders, monseigneur. We are ready to die for you.
Let us wait.
If we endeavor to fly, they will sink us.

Night came on...

...as did the French warship.

A rope-ladder was thrown over the side...and Aramis boldly boarded the larger vessel.

The surprise of the Breton sailors was great when they saw him walk straight up to the commander...

...and make a mysterious sign to him.

Five minutes later, Aramis emerged with the captain from his cabin...

Point the head of the ship toward Corunna*...

*A Spanish port.

That night saw Aramis leaning upon the bulwarks...

...and witnessed, perhaps, the first tears had ever fallen from his eyes.

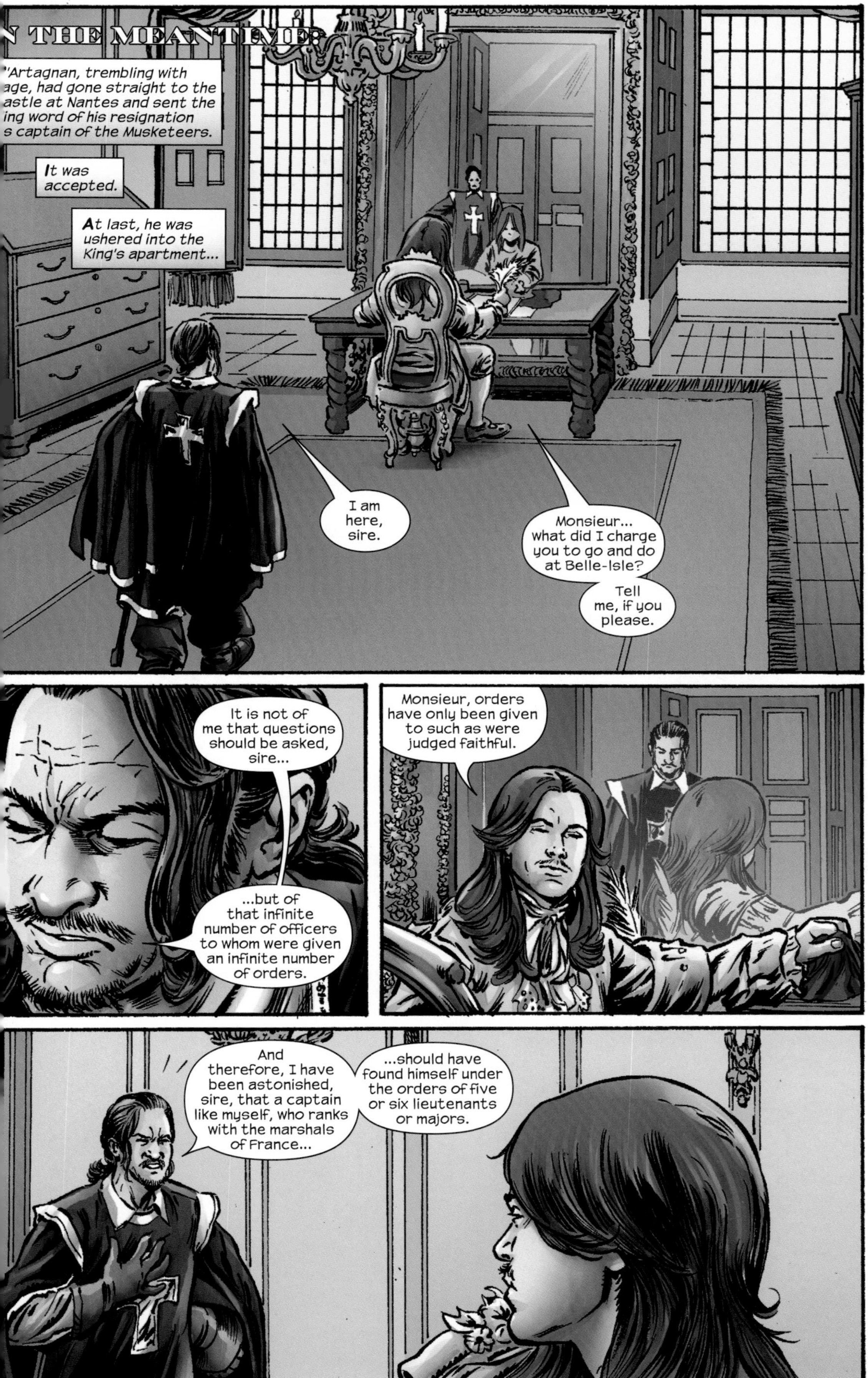
N THE MEANTIME:
'Artagnan, trembling with age, had gone straight to the astle at Nantes and sent the ing word of his resignation s captain of the Musketeers.
It was accepted.
At last, he was ushered into the King's apartment...
I am here, sire.
Monsieur... what did I charge you to go and do at Belle-Isle?
Tell me, if you please.
It is not of me that questions should be asked, sire...
...but of that infinite number of officers to whom were given an infinite number of orders.
Monsieur, orders have only been given to such as were judged faithful.
And therefore, I have been astonished, sire, that a captain like myself, who ranks with the marshals of France...
...should have found himself under the orders of five or six lieutenants or majors.

It was such insults, offered to a brave man, that led me to respectfully offer Your Majesty my resignation.

And I have accepted it, monsieur.

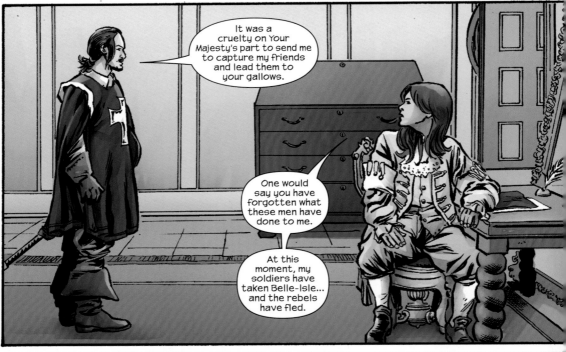

It was a cruelty on Your Majesty's part to send me to capture my friends and lead them to your gallows.

One would say you have forgotten what these men have done to me.

At this moment, my soldiers have taken Belle-Isle... and the rebels have fled.

Lofty heads have bowed to me, Monsieur d'Artagnan.

Bow yours... or choose the exile that will best suit you.

Are you content, sire?

Reckoning from today, I have no longer any enemies in France.

It remains with me to send you to a foreign field to gather your marshal's baton.*

Depend upon me for finding you an opportunity.

* To gain France's highest military office by winning victories abroad.

t is all d and ell!

But-- those poor men at Belle-Isle-- one, in particular, so good...so brave... so true!

Do you ask their pardon of me?

Upon my knees, sire.

Well! Then go and take it to them, if it be still time.

But do you answer for their behavior in the future?

With my life, sire!

And, with a heart swelling with joy, d'Artagnan rushed out of the castle, on his way to Belle-Isle.

But he would soon learn that Porthos was dead, and that Aramis had escaped to the territories of the King of Spain.

At his old friend's baronial estate, some days later, d'Artagnan listened to the reading of Porthos' will...

"...and, having no relations, I have left all my property to M. le Vicomte Raoul Auguste Jules de Bragelonne..."

Raoul--son of their mutual friend Athos, Count de la Fère.

Raoul--who has gone to Africa with the hope of dying in combat.

Athos, meanwhile, had become an old man in a week, upon receiving a letter from Aramis, in Spain...

Porthos is dead!

I dreamed last night that dear Raoul came to me, and told me as much.

Oh, Raoul--Raoul! Thou keepest thy promise!

Thou warnes me!

Then Athos felt his head become confused. his legs give way...

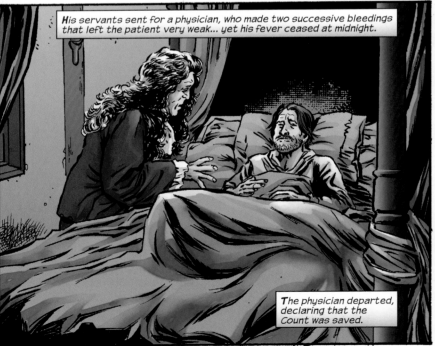

His servants sent for a physician, who made two successive bleedings that left the patient very weak... yet his fever ceased at midnight.

The physician departed, declaring that the Count was saved.

Then commenced for Athos a strange, indefinable state...

Free to think, his mind turned towards his beloved son...

Raoul...

His imagination painted the fields of Africa in the environs of Gigelli,* where the Duke de Beaufort must have landed his army and fought a battle.

An inexpressible shudder of horror seized him to recognize the uniform of the soldiers of Picardy...

...saw all the gaping, cold wounds looking up to the azure heavens as if to demand back from them the souls to which they had opened a passage...

*Modern-day Sierra Leone.

...saw the body of M. de Beaufort, in the first ranks of the dead.

Then he saw a white form appear...

Raoul.

The Count attempted to utter a cry...

But it remained stifled in his throat.

And as he gained the crest of the hill, he beheld his son rising into the void...

...departing toward heaven...

...when the charm was suddenly broken.

RAOUL...!

Athos did not stir as he heard a horse galloping through his gates...

He scarcely turned his head as a heavy step ascended the stairs...

He beheld his son's servant, who had accompanied him to Africa...

Grimaud...!

Yes, Monsieur le Comte.

Raoul is dead, is he not?

Yes.

HERE I AM!

Athos, my friend!...

Monsieur le Chevalier d'Artagnan!

Where is he?

Where...?

He died... when he learned of his son's death.

Adieu, old friend...

D'Artagnan arose, tearing himself from the chamber where he had just found dead...

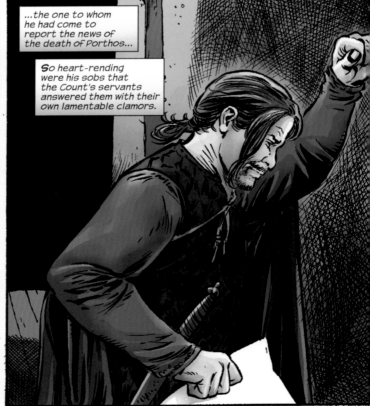

...the one to whom he had come to report the news of the death of Porthos...

So heart-rending were his sobs that the Count's servants answered them with their own lamentable clamors.

At daybreak, Grimaud gave d'Artagnan a letter written by M. de Beaufort before he himself had died...

My Dear Count--

Amidst a great triumph, your son, M. de Bragelonne, has died gloriously.

After his death in battle, we discovered a lock of fair hair in his right hand...and that hand was pressed tightly upon his heart.

Your good friend,

Le Duc de Beaufort

Oh, unhappy boy! A suicide!

But they have kept their words to each other-- and are now reunited.

On the morrow, the cold remains of both father and son--whose body had been embalmed that he might be buried in France--were returned to the earth...

I shall follow thy funerals, my friends-- I, already old--I, who am of no value on earth...

And I shall scatter dust upon those brows.

Left alone at last to bid a last adieu to the double grave which contained his two lost friends, d'Artagnan forgot the hour, while thinking of the dead...

And he heard a woman praying...and weeping.

≈Sobbb...≈

Mademoiselle de la Vallière! You--*here*?

M. d'Artagnan...

I should better have liked to see you decked with flowers in the mansion of the Comte de la Fère!

You would have wept less-- I, too!

I know I have caused the death of the Vicomte de Bragelonne...and thereby, his father.

But... I must go. The King's carriage awaits.

You see, madam, that your happiness still lasts.

A day will come, monsieur, when you will repent of having so ill-judged me.

For Raoul, I would have given my *life* without hesitation...

But I could not give my *love*.

M. Fouquet cannot comprehend that banishment is liberty, falconer...

...any more than I can get used to being called a "Count," even after four years.

Is M. Fouquet well, Monsieur le Comte?

He had a near chance of the scaffold, before the King merely banished him.

I left the court mourning the death of the Queen-Mother...

And Louise de Vallière was right...

I *do* feel pity for her, now that she has been replaced by another in the King's affections.

M. Colbert* approaches, monsieur...

*Louis XIV's finance minister.

Good day, M. d'Artagnan. Have you had a pleasant journey?

Yes, monsieur.

The King wishes to invite you to his table for this evening.

You will meet an old friend there...

...M. le Duc d'Alméda, who is arrived this morning from Spain.

A Spanish duke--an old friend of mine?

I!

Perhaps *now* you will recognize me...

Aramis!

So you, the exile, are again in France!

And I shall dine with you at the King's table.

M. Colbert, as minister of finance, was kind enough to arrange it.

It was my pleasure, Monsieur le Duc.

He counts upon my influence to keep Spain neutral in the coming war with the United Provinces.*

King Louis' favorite new game is war.

His greed has expanded beyond the boundaries of France.

He even wants to ally with the English King Charles, so he can have the support of the English Navy in a war against the Dutch.

It is a war which, otherwise, the French would be ill-prepared to fight.

*The Netherlands.

It is all very well to make sure France has ships--but it will still need a fine army, finely led...

...or else, in the Dutch lands, soldiers will be drowned for want of a boat, a plank, or a stick.

But then, it is my profession to die for His Majesty.

I never heard of an instance of a marshal of France being drowned, d'Artagnan.

I--a marshal of France?

A man must have commanded an expedition in chief to obtain the baton.

I have brought you a plan of a campaign you will lead a body of troops to carry out in the next spring.

I implore you to tell the King that he may depend upon a victory, or seeing me dead.

Then I will have the fleur-de-lis for your marshal's baton prepared immediately.

And you will, perhaps, never see me again, dear d'Artagnan.

I am old...

I am extinguished...

I am dead.

My friend, you will live longer than I shall.

Diplomacy commands you to live...but for my part, honor condemns me to die.

Bah! Such men as we are, Monsieur le Marshal, only die satiated with joy or glory.

I assure you, Monsieur le Duc, I feel very little appetite for either.

Let us love each other for four...

...though we are now but two.

*T*wo hours later, they were separated.

*S*oon, with Spain neutral, the English Navy, ballasted by a few millions of French gold, made a devastating campaign against the Dutch fleets.

*I*n the spring, M. d'Artagnan's army of 12,000 men took twelve places in northern Holland within a month...

...and he was in the fifth day of a siege against the thirteenth.

The reconstruction of the trenches is complete, M. d'Artagnan.

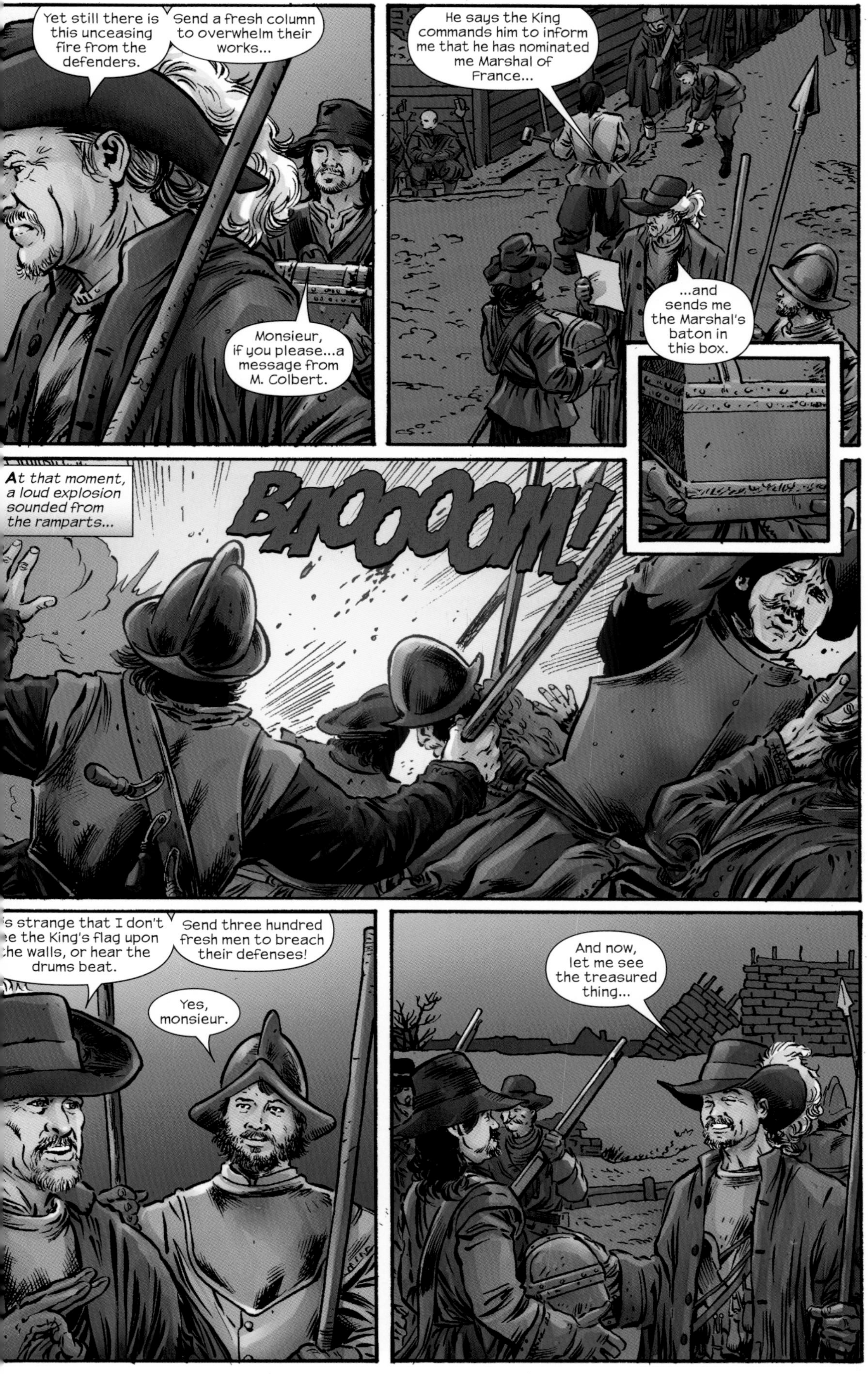
Yet still there is this unceasing fire from the defenders.
Send a fresh column to overwhelm their works...
Monsieur, if you please...a message from M. Colbert.
He says the King commands him to inform me that he has nominated me Marshal of France...
...and sends me the Marshal's baton in this box.
At that moment, a loud explosion sounded from the ramparts...
BROOOOM!
's strange that I don't ee the King's flag upon he walls, or hear the drums beat.
Send three hundred fresh men to breach their defenses!
Yes, monsieur.
And now, let me see the treasured thing...

...that M. Colbert has sent.

BAOOOOM!!

The ball from the city crushed the box in the arms of the officer...

...struck d'Artagnan full in the chest...

...and knocked him down...

...upon a sloping heap of earth.

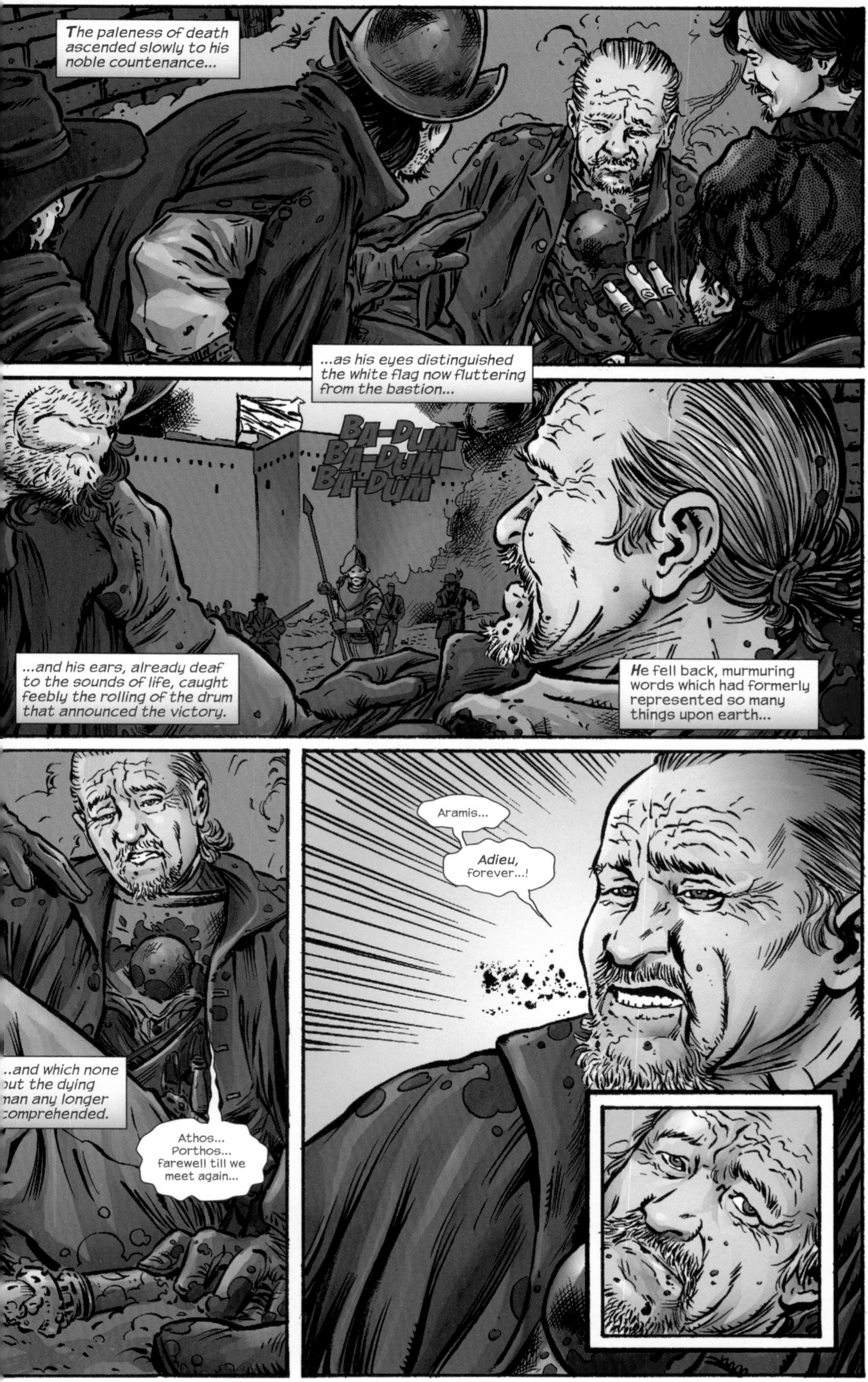
The paleness of death ascended slowly to his noble countenance...
...as his eyes distinguished the white flag now fluttering from the bastion...
BA-DUM BA-DUM BA-DUM
...and his ears, already deaf to the sounds of life, caught feebly the rolling of the drum that announced the victory.
He fell back, murmuring words which had formerly represented so many things upon earth...
...and which none but the dying man any longer comprehended.
Athos... Porthos... farewell till we meet again...
Aramis...
Adieu, forever...!

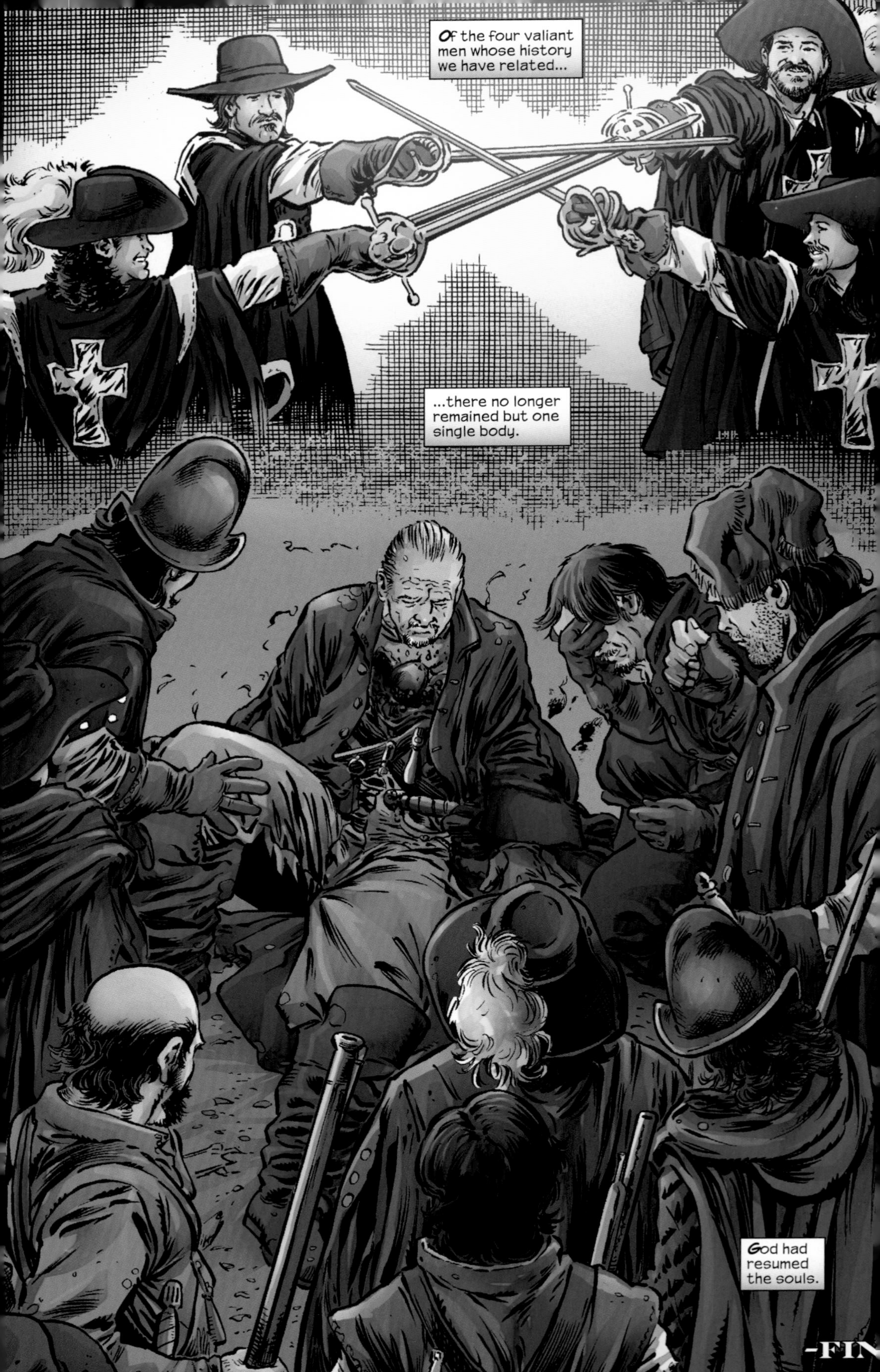
Of the four valiant men whose history we have related...
...there no longer remained but one single body.
God had resumed the souls.
-FIN